Adam Raccoon
and the
Mighty Giant

Glen Keane

Chariot Books™
David C. Cook Publishing Co.

To
Mom and Dad
For their love, humor,
and encouragement

Chariot Books™ is an imprint of David C. Cook Publishing Co.
David C. Cook Publishing Co., Elgin, Illinois 60120
David C. Cook Publishing Co., Weston, Ontario

ADAM RACCOON AND THE MIGHTY GIANT
© 1989 by Glen Keane for text and illustrations

Scripture quoted from the *International Children's Bible, New Century Version,* copyright © 1986 by Sweet Publishing, Fort Worth, Texas 76137. Used by permission.

First printing, 1989

94 93 92   5 4

Library of Congress Cataloging-in-Publication Data

Keane, Glen, 1954-
  Adam Raccoon and the mighty giant / Glen Keane.
    p. cm.—(Parables for kids)
  Summary: When a giant invades Master's Wood, Adam Racoon is the one animal chosen by King Aren to welcome the frightening visitor and tell him who is king.
  ISBN 1-55513-288-X
  [1. Giants—Fiction. 2. Raccoons—Fiction. 3. Animals—Fiction. 4. Kings, queens, rulers, etc.—Fiction. 5. Parables.]
I. Title. II. Series: Keane, Glen, 1954- Parables for kids.
PZ7.K2173Ack   1989
[E]—dc19   89-31229
                                                   CIP
                                                   AC

A mighty roar echoed through Master's Wood.

It was King Aren
calling for Adam Raccoon.

CRACK

SNAP

Soon the forest
rustled behind him.

"You called, King Aren?" Adam wheezed as he stumbled out.

"Yes, Adam.
Here, sit down
and catch your breath.

"This is all my kingdom, Adam,
but not all know me as their king.

"I want you to
go and tell them."

Adam thought for a moment, then said, "I will, King Aren. You can count on me!"

"Good! Here's your badge. You are
now my deputy."

"Whoopee!" Adam shouted as he ran down the mountain. "Thank you, King Aren!"

Later that day as Adam was
showing everybody his badge . . .

The ground started to shake.

Towering high above the treetops,
a giant thundered through
Master's Wood.
Boom! Boom!

BOOM

The animals all scattered.

Boom! Boom! Boom!
The giant stomped off
into the distance.

"Gather 'round everybody!" King Aren shouted. "Don't be afraid of the giant.

"We need someone to go and welcome him to Master's Wood and tell him I am the king."

"Uh oh, that means me,"
Adam thought.

"Adam, will you go?"
King Aren asked.

"I, uh . . . really . . . I'd rather not.
You see, . . .
I'm just a little guy and he's so
big!"

And everyone else said the same thing—except Freddy the Frog.

"How about you, Freddy?"

"I'm not afraid of a giant! I'll go!"
he boasted.

The crowd cheered and the band
played as Freddy marched off.

But as soon as he was out of sight he hid. "I'm not lookin' for a giant!" he said.

Meanwhile Adam sat staring at his badge,

remembering King Aren's words,
"Not all know me as
their king."

"The giant needs to know!" Adam
said, and off he ran to find him.

Through the darkening forest
Adam searched.

But he could not
see the giant.
Then suddenly . . .

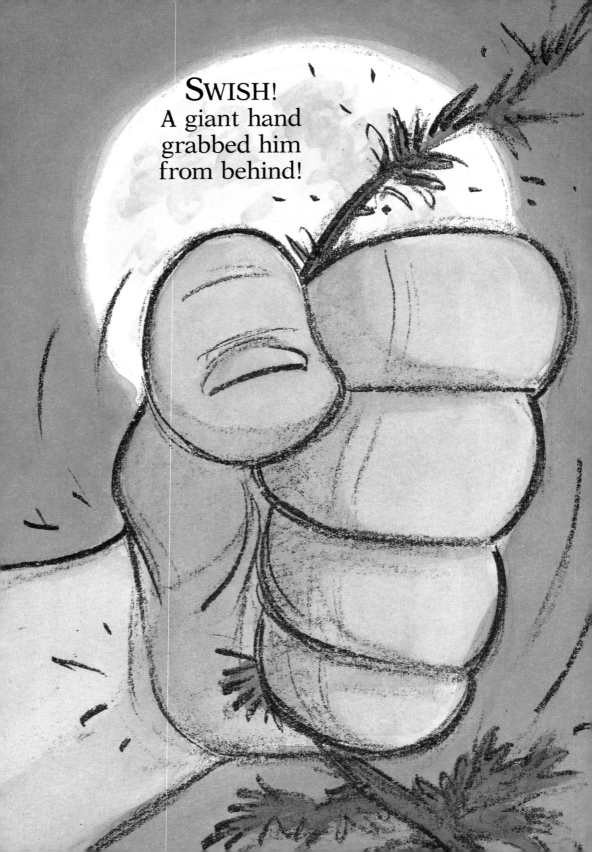

SWISH!
A giant hand
grabbed him
from behind!

"W-W-Welcome to Master's Wood, Mr. Giant," Adam stuttered.

"I came to tell you about
our king."

And the giant listened as Adam told him about the wise and loving King Aren.

Meanwhile, King Aren had been
looking for Adam when . . .

BOOM BOOM BOOM

The ground started shaking again.

"Run! It's the giant!" the animals screamed.

"No, wait. Look!" King Aren
shouted.

"Don't be frightened. He wants to meet King Aren."

"Welcome to Master's Wood,"
King Aren said as they
shook hands.

There was a great party
that night to welcome the giant.
Everyone was there . . .